My Little Book of

Burrowing Owls

By Hope Irvin Marston
Illustrated by Maria Magdalena Brown

Windward Publishing

AN IMPRINT OF FINNEY COMPANY
www.finney-hobar.com

One spring evening two burrowing owls
skimmed over the grasslands.

SWOOOP!

Down they dropped to an empty
prairie dog burrow.

They crept inside and looked around their old nest. Another animal had lived in it over the winter, and it was a mess.

The owls would clean it up.

PECK!   PECK!   **PECK!**

The busy little birds poked at the walls with their beaks.

SWISH!   **SWISH!**

The male bird kicked the dirt backward toward the burrow opening. Out flew little puffs of dirt.

When the owl stopped to rest, his mate finished the cleaning.

That night the owls stood on the mound outside the burrow. They bent their gangly legs and bowed to each other.

"Cu~coo. Cu~coo," sang the male.

The owls snuggled throughout the night. Sometimes they rubbed each other's bills. And they preened each other's feathers. When the male saw a field mouse in the grass, he brought it to his mate for a midnight snack.

The next day the owls lined their nest with feathers
and dead grass. And with dried cow manure.

They left some manure outside the burrow.
The smell would help keep hungry badgers or snakes away
from their babies.

During the next two weeks, the female laid seven eggs.
She turned the eggs often to keep them warm beneath her.
Twice a day she hopped up to the entrance for food.

"*Rasssp! Rasssp!*" She called to her mate.

He flew to her with insects. Or birds. Or mice.

The first egg hatched on the twenty-eighth day.

Peck! Peck!

Scritch! Scratch!

Day after day another little owlet no bigger than your thumb pipped its shell with its beak.

Each of the seven helpless new owlets opened its eyes when it was five days old.

Crack! Craack! Craaack!

When the owlets were about two weeks old, they hobbled out of the crowded burrow. They huddled in the bright sunlight near the entrance.

"KOOK-COO!" "KOOK-COO!"

They sounded like tiny roosters trying to crow.

They wanted to be fed.

Down swooped their father with a small garter
snake. The owlets rushed at him on their spindly legs.

They grabbed the snake from his beak and
gobbled it up.

The parents worked hard finding food for the
hungry little chicks.

When they were
three weeks old, the owlets
could run.

And hop.

And preen.

And flap their wings.

It was time to learn to hunt for their own food.

Their father taught them to catch grasshoppers and other bugs.

One morning the owlets sat in the sun near the burrow. Suddenly, the mother owl began to bob her body. She swiveled her head. **"Tweee-chikit- chikit- chikit- chik!"** she warned.

A fox was creeping closer and closer.

"*Eep! Eep! Eep!*" cried the owlets as they hurried into the burrow. Their mother rushed in right behind them.

As the fox came toward the burrow, it heard,

"Hissszzzzz! HissssZZZZZZZ! HISSSZZZZZ!"

It sounded like a rattlesnake. The fox turned and ran back across the prairie.

The little owls had scared the fox away. It didn't know frightened burrowing owls hissed like rattlesnakes.

When it was safe, the owlets came
out of the burrow.

They s-t-r-e-t-c-h-e-d themselves.
They chased beetles and bugs and crickets. They flapped their wings. They made funny little leaps into the air, but they couldn't fly yet.

The owls did learn to fly by the time they were six weeks old. Still, they stayed near the burrow. They perched on fence posts to watch for prey on the ground.

They flew over the field in search of grasshoppers. And locusts. And dragonflies. When they found some, they grabbed them with their talons.

The parent owls sat on the ground and fluffed their feathers. They pushed their faces into the loose soil.

Pffffffft! Pffffffft! Pffffffft!

They swiveled their heads, scattering the dirt.

By bathing in the dust, they got rid of loose feathers. And fleas. And mites. Soon the seven owlets were dust bathing, too.

As the owlets grew, their nest became too crowded. One by one they moved into empty burrows of their own nearby.

One fall morning, frost covered the ground. A cold wind blew.

The owls had trouble finding food. It was time to leave the northern prairie. Now they must fly south to warm weather. And lizards. And bugs. In the spring, they will return to raise families of their own.

DEDICATIONS:

FOR LUKE, SARAH, AND RUTHIE
– H.I.M.

FOR ALAN
– M.M.B.

ACKNOWLEDGMENT:

The author wishes to thank Mr. Denver W. Holt and Ms. Kila Jarvis of the Owl Research Institute, Inc., Missoula, Montana, for their kind assistance and advice.

ISBN 0-89317-054-2
Second Edition, First Published by NorthWord Press 1996

This book is part of the My Little Book series.
For other titles in this series, visit www.finney-hobar.com or your favorite bookseller.

Windward Publishing
3943 Meadowbrook Road
Minneapolis, MN 55426-4505

AN IMPRINT OF FINNEY COMPANY

www.finney-hobar.com

Printed in the United States of America